BY JAKE MADDOX

illustrated by Sean Tiffany

text by Bob Temple

Librarian Reviewer
Chris Kreie
Media Specialist, Eden Prairie Schools, MN
MS in Information Media, St. Cloud State University, MN

Reading Consultant
Mary Evenson
Middle School Teacher, Edina Public Schools, MN
MA in Education, University of Minnesota

STONE ARCH BOOKS
Minneapolis   San Diego

Jake Maddox Books are published by Stone Arch Books,
A Capstone Imprint
1710 Roe Crest Drive,
North Mankato, Minnesota 56003
www.capstonepub.com

Library of Congress Cataloging-in-Publication Data

Maddox, Jake.
    Board Rebel / by Jake Maddox; illustrated by Sean Tiffany.
    p. cm. — (A Jake Maddox Sports Story)
    Summary: When Tanner moves to an exclusive new town he misses
his old skate park, but with the help of the town bully and another new
friend, Tanner thinks he can figure out a way to get a skate park built in
Woodville.
    ISBN-13: 978-1-59889-319-9 (library binding)
    ISBN-10: 1-59889-319-X (library binding)
    ISBN-13: 978-1-59889-414-1 (paperback)
    ISBN-10: 1-59889-414-5 (paperback)
    [1. Skateboarding—Fiction. 2. Moving, Household—Fiction.]
I. Tiffany, Sean, ill. II. Title.
PZ7.M25643Bo 2007
[Fic]—dc22   2006027806

Art Director: Heather Kindseth
Graphic Designer: Kay Fraser

Printed in the United States of America.
022318 000215

TABLE OF CONTENTS

Chapter 1

King of the Park

Tanner Ryan tipped the front edge of his skateboard over the lip of the ramp. His back foot held the board in place by its tail. His front foot tapped at the battered front edge of the board.

Tanner looked down at the board. All the slides and grinds he had done over the last year had left his board in bad shape. Time for a new one, he thought. But I'm sure that won't happen until my birthday.

Two more months. It would be hard to wait. It might even be harder for him to part with the board that helped him win his first Citywide Skateboard Challenge, however.

Tanner's eyes scanned over the other, younger skaters as they whipped around the park. The little guys rode back and forth between the smallest ramps.

Tanner smiled. It wasn't that long ago that he was one of those little guys. Now he was standing at the top of the biggest half-pipe in the city.

"Hey, Tanner, what are you waiting for?" came a voice from the other end of the pipe. It was Billy Collins, one of Tanner's best skateboarding buddies. "Let's see what you got today!"

Tanner grinned. "A lot more than what you got, that's for sure," he called.

With that, he tipped the board forward and rode it down the ramp. He was headed straight for Billy, who was standing at the top of the opposite side of the ramp. Tanner's grin grew as his board climbed the far edge of the pipe.

Tanner barreled off the top edge of the pipe. He flew up, turned a perfect three-sixty in front of Billy's face, and dropped easily back down into the half-pipe. "Eat that!" Tanner called back to Billy.

Billy laughed, then jumped down the half-pipe, trailing after Tanner. They spent the rest of the day chasing each other and trying out new tricks. Each boy would try something new, and the other would quickly try to match it.

By the end of the day, they were pretty tired and really sore. Even with all of their protective gear on, they still came away with some bumps and bruises. Tanner's pants, already ripped up from a number of falls, had some new damage.

Finally, it was time to head home. Tanner and Billy headed off together, grinding on curbs and jumping over sidewalk cracks and anything else they could find. About a block away from Tanner's house, Billy turned down a different street. "Catch you later," he said.

"You'll never catch me," Tanner said, laughing.

Tanner wheeled for home. He was still the best skater at the park. But he didn't know about the surprise that was waiting for him at home.

Chapter 2

The Big Surprise

Tanner wheeled around to the back of the house. He popped his board up into his right hand, swung open the screen door, and walked inside.

"Tanner? Is that you?" his dad called from the kitchen. "Come in here, quick! We've got a big surprise for you!"

At last! Tanner thought to himself. They finally decided to get me a new skateboard!

Tanner turned the corner and walked into the kitchen. He glanced around the room quickly.

There was no new skateboard that he could see. But both of his parents smiled broadly at him. Tanner stood in the doorway.

Something was up. Normally, food would be getting cooked and his parents would be asking him about his day.

Instead, they just looked at him, smiling. "What's going on?" Tanner asked. "You guys are acting, um, weird."

"We've got big news," Tanner's dad said. "I'm getting promoted at work."

"Oh, cool," Tanner said.

"Tanner," his mom said. "This is really good news. Your dad worked hard for this."

"Oh, I know," Tanner said. He struggled to sound more excited about it. "I mean, that's great. Good job, Dad." Tanner felt uncomfortable. He tried to leave the room.

"Tanner, wait," his mom said. "There's more. Dad's going to be working in a different office," she said. "Out in Woodville. Out by my office."

"Oh, that's cool," Tanner said to his mom. "You'll have company on the drive."

Again, Tanner turned to leave. Finally, his parents couldn't hold it in any more.

"Um, Tanner," his mom said, "it's not going to be a long drive."

There was a pause. Tanner started to realize that he might not like what was coming next.

"We're moving," his dad said.

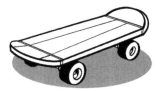

Chapter 3

The New House

It seemed like Tanner had no time to get ready. In a matter of a month, the house had been sold and he was moving. He could hardly believe it was happening.

Woodville was only an hour away. It might have been a million miles to Tanner. He wouldn't be close to his friend Billy. He wouldn't be close to the city skate park he loved. He wouldn't be close to anyone he knew.

His parents bought a fancy new house in a very nice neighborhood.

It was nothing like what Tanner was used to. The new house was a two-story. Tanner's bedroom was about twice as big as his old bedroom.

There was a separate room that his parents had set up as a game room for Tanner. It had a big-screen TV for video games and a pool table.

Tanner's parents put the family computer in that room too. Tanner knew he'd spend a lot of time in there.

The best part of the new house was in the backyard. It was a giant swimming pool.

On the night they moved in, Tanner turned on his computer.

When he discovered Billy was online, he sent him an instant message.

"U wouldn't believe my new house," Tanner wrote.

"Big?" Billy wrote back.

"It's sweet," Tanner wrote. "Pool and game room. You should come see it."

"Lucky," Billy wrote.

Tanner wasn't so sure. True, his new surroundings were nothing like his old neighborhood. But that was part of the problem. Tanner didn't quite feel comfortable in the new neighborhood.

Every day after school, Tanner hopped on his skateboard and explored the area. He rode up and down the streets. He grinded on the curbs. He practiced his kick flips, his ollies and his one-eighties.

There was no skate park to be found. What he did find were beautiful lawns and perfect flower gardens. Worse, some of the sidewalks and crosswalks were made of stone. That made it very tough to skateboard.

Near some of the shops in town, he found some steps and railings he could use to do tricks. When he tried to do them during the day, however, the store owners told him to stop.

Tanner was lonely. Instant-messaging with Billy wasn't helping either.

"There was a new kid at the park today," Billy wrote one night. "He was pretty good."

"Nobody here skates," Tanner wrote. After three weeks, Tanner hadn't made any friends.

Chapter 4

One night after dinner, the doorbell rang. Tanner got up from the computer and headed toward the steps.

When he reached the top of the steps, he saw that his mom had already answered the door. She was talking to a woman in a fancy dress. Tanner recognized her.

The woman lived down the street. One day when Tanner was skateboarding, the woman had yelled at him.

She'd told him to stay off her property. Tanner was pretty sure that her visit wasn't to welcome them to the neighborhood.

Tanner tried to listen, but he couldn't hear everything.

"It's got to stop," he heard the woman say. "The vote was unanimous."

Tanner's mom was nice to the woman, but Tanner could tell she was not happy. She invited the woman in, but the woman said she was on her way to a concert.

When the woman left, Tanner started down the stairs.

"What's she talking about, Mom?" Tanner said.

Tanner's mom looked sad. "Well, we've got a little problem," she said.

"Let's go into the living room and talk about it as a family."

Tanner didn't like the sound of that, either. It had to be bad news.

"That was Mrs. Parsons," Tanner's mom said. "She's the chairperson of our neighborhood committee."

"Yeah?" Tanner said. "So what?"

"She said that the committee is upset with the marks that your skateboard leaves on the curbs and sidewalks," Tanner's mom said. "And the store managers are upset about you riding the railings by the shopping area."

"Too bad for them," Tanner said. "It's a free country."

"That's true, but we all have to live by the rules," Tanner's dad said.

He paused and looked at Tanner. "Woodville's a controlled community. When you live here, you agree to follow the neighborhood covenants."

"What does that mean?" Tanner asked.

"It means that we all agree to follow the rules that the committee makes," Tanner's mom said. "Unfortunately, at their meeting tonight, they agreed to a new rule."

"What's that?" Tanner asked.

"No skateboarding on city streets," his mom said.

Chapter 5

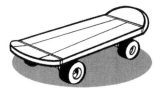

Finding the Curves

The next morning, Tanner woke up feeling determined. He strapped his skateboard on the back of his bike and took off.

He wasn't going to return until he found a place to skateboard — a place where no one could tell him he couldn't.

His plan was to get outside the city of Woodville. He hoped that a neighboring city might be less strict about its rules.

He didn't have to go very far. About a half mile away, he came across a park.

He knew he was still in Woodville, but the park looked like a great place to skate. There were curving, paved paths winding all around.

It's still in Woodville, he thought. But these paths aren't city streets. They can't stop me from skateboarding here.

Then he saw it.

On the far left side of the park, there was a large hill. From top to bottom, the hill featured a long, winding path. It was perfectly paved, with a mixture of sharp, hairpin turns and big downhill drops. The path wound its way through a flower garden with a fountain and a statue of one of the city's founders.

Tanner could imagine the adults in the city taking long, slow walks through this beautiful park in the evenings. On a nice summer weekday like this one, however, the paths were empty. A few small children played in the playground area with a parent, but no one was using the paths.

In a flash, Tanner rode his bike to the highest point of the path. He stood there, straddling his bike, wondering if he dared try to ride down the sloping path.

From the top, parts of the path looked more like cliffs. Every turn looked more dangerous and exciting than the one before it.

Tanner swung his right leg off his bike. He quickly began untying his skateboard from the back. Then he heard a voice.

"Hey, kid."

Tanner wheeled around. There were three boys approaching from behind him. They were all neatly dressed. Tanner wondered what they thought of him in his ripped jeans and ratty T-shirt.

"What do you think you are doing?" said the tall one in the middle.

Tanner pushed his brown curls away from his eyes. "What's it to you?" he said.

The three boys walked up to Tanner. None of them smiled. The middle one took off his backpack and set it aside.

Tanner wasn't worried about a fight. They were dressed too nice to get dirty. He looked at the middle boy's backpack. Monogrammed on the front pocket was "BP III."

"This is our park, that's what," the middle one said. "Where do you live?"

"Just over that way," Tanner said, pointing in the direction of his house. "About a half mile. We just moved in."

"You must be that skateboarder who's got everybody mad," the boy said. "You've got a few things to learn about Woodville."

"Like what?" Tanner asked.

"Like nobody skateboards here," he said.

"Well," Tanner said, "I do."

"Not down the Curves, you don't," the boy said.

"The Curves?" Tanner said. "So it has a name, huh? Are you telling me no one's ever skateboarded down the Curves?"

"That's right," the boy said. "And you won't either."

"Sorry," Tanner said, "you're wrong about that, too."

Tanner was on his skateboard and on his way down the hill before anyone could move. The first few turns were easy. As he careened down the hill, he picked up speed. He was fine on the first few turns, but he found himself getting closer to the edges with each corner.

The final turn was the hardest. It was a sharp turn. Tanner leaned in hard as he made the turn. He stretched his arms out and bent his knees to help keep his balance.

His back wheels wobbled. Tanner wavered, but stayed up on the board. Finally, he reached the last straightaway. He pumped his fist above his head.

It was the first time he had felt good about his new home.

Chapter 6

Bennett Parsons III

Despite the long uphill walk to the top of the Curves, Tanner's smile never left his face. The three boys at the top were smiling too.

"Not bad," the one in the middle said. "I'm Bennett Parsons the Third."

Suddenly, Tanner knew what "BP III" on the backpack meant. "This is Will," Bennett said, gesturing to the boy on the left. "And this is Brock."

"Hey," Tanner said, nodding to the boys. There was an uncomfortable pause, then Tanner spoke up. "So, none of you guys skateboard?"

Will started to answer, but Bennett interrupted. "Ah, no," he scoffed. "We don't. Better things to do."

"Whatever you say, BP Three," Tanner said. "But you're missing out."

"The name is Bennett," he said. "No one calls me anything but Bennett."

"Okay," Tanner said. Tanner fussed with his skateboard. He tugged at a little sliver of wood that was falling off one edge.

The three boys huddled briefly. Then Bennett spoke up.

"That was a pretty good ride," he said. "You should try the railings."

Tanner glanced down the hill. About halfway down the Curves, in between two of the hairpin switchbacks, was a small stone staircase. The steps went right between the fountain and the statue.

Alongside the steps were two sets of railings. There was gap of about three feet between the railings.

"It would be pretty cool to see you do the Curves and the rails," Bennett said. "If you can do that, you might be able to fit in around here."

Tanner eyed the challenge. He knew it wouldn't be easy. "I'm not interested in fitting in around here," Tanner said. "But I'll do it anyway."

Bennett and Brock grinned. Tanner knew they wanted him to blow it.

Then Tanner caught Will's eye. Will looked worried.

Tanner smiled. "Tell you what, BP Three," he said. Bennett's grin disappeared. "If I make it down the rails, how about you give it a try?"

Bennett rolled his eyes. "Fine," he said.

Tanner took off. He found the going easier on the turns this time. He learned from his first trip down, and this second ride was much smoother. He kept his eyes focused on the rails as they grew nearer.

Tanner cut a sharp turn to the left, crossing back. One turn remained before the rails. He braced himself as he turned back right.

He got ready for the jump up to the first rail. He'd done rails a million times.

But he had never done it at this speed, and he'd never done it on this steep of an incline.

Tanner pumped down on his board and popped it up as he leaped for the first rail. He went for a front-side board slide. The front wheels would go over the rail, and the middle of his board would slide down the rail.

Tanner's left foot was forward. He would take the first rail facing the top of the hill, then try a one-eighty turn and take the second rail down.

The board seemed to stick to the bottom of his feet. It looked perfect. Tanner popped up on the first rail.

"Wow!" Will exclaimed. Bennett shot him an angry glance.

Tanner felt a rush of confidence. He had nailed it. He eyed the boys at the top of the hill and gave them a little grin. When he looked back to the rail, however, the gap was approaching faster than he thought.

His legs pumped to try to get some air so he could cover the gap. But he was too late. The board was already coming off the first rail, and he didn't get the push he needed to make it to the second one.

As he tried to make the one-eighty turn, his left foot slipped off the board. Now he was spinning, falling, crashing. His left ankle smacked into the railing. The board bounced off the rail and hit him in the face. He tried to grab the rail with his arm but missed.

He landed hard in the flowerbed, but he was going too fast to stop quickly.

He tumbled through roses and tulips before a thick shrub snagged him just in time to keep him from hitting the next section of the paved path.

Tanner lay on his stomach, motionless. His ankle throbbed. He was scraped and bruised and battered. He was bleeding from tiny punctures and scrapes the rose bushes provided.

Tanner rolled to his back and looked to the top of the hill.

The boys were gone.

Chapter 7

That night, as Tanner's mom plucked thorns from the rose bushes out of Tanner's arms and legs, the doorbell rang. Tanner's dad went to the door. Tanner couldn't hear the conversation, but he did know who his dad was talking to: Mrs. Parsons.

"That didn't take long," Tanner muttered.

"What do you mean?" Tanner's mom said.

"I'm sure BP Three went straight home and told his mommy what happened," Tanner said.

"Tanner!" his mom said. "I'm surprised at you. That boy may have egged you on, but you're the one who tried it."

Tanner's head sank. He knew she was right. It didn't really matter to him, though. To Tanner, the day's events were just more proof that he didn't belong in this neighborhood. Then his dad came in with the news.

"Well, Tanner," his dad said, "they've banned skateboarding in the park, too. And they gave me a bill for the repairs."

Tanner stood up, his shoulders sinking, and wandered up the stairs toward his bedroom.

The next morning, Tanner's dad greeted him with a surprise. "Hey, Tanner, get up and get dressed," he said. "I need to run back to the old neighborhood. I'll drop you at the skate park if you like."

Tanner was out of bed like a shot. The bumps and bruises from the day before still ached, but he pretended not to notice. In just a few minutes, he had his clothes on and his skateboard in his hand, and was headed out the door.

The drive to the park seemed to take forever. Tanner couldn't wait. When they arrived at the park, Tanner popped out of the car. "I'll be back at four," his dad said. "That's six hours."

"Okay, Dad!" Tanner replied. He dropped his board to the ground and rolled off to the park. "See you."

Tanner could see Billy at the half-pipe. He skated over there as fast as he could. Billy tipped over the edge and started down the pipe before he heard Tanner.

"Yo, Billy," Tanner yelped. "Let's see what you've got today!"

Billy was so shocked that he lost his balance at the bottom of the half-pipe and fell off his board.

"Not much, by the look of it!" Tanner said.

Billy wasn't hurt. "Hey, man!" Billy said. "What are you doing here? Are you moving back?"

"I wish," Tanner said. They bumped fists and headed up toward the top of the half-pipe. Tanner explained that he was just stopping in for the day.

Off they went. They tracked each other, trying new tricks and challenging each other.

In the middle of the afternoon, Tanner noticed another boy about his age across the park. "That's the new kid," Billy said. "He's only here on weekends. He's kind of quiet, but he seems okay."

Something was familiar about the boy, Tanner thought. It was hard to tell in the helmet and pads, but he thought he might know him. There was no question he was a good skater. Everything he tried looked very natural. As the boy got closer, Tanner caught a glimpse of his face.

"Holy cow," Tanner said as the boy approached. "It's you!"

Chapter 8

A New Plan

"Will, right?" Tanner said to the boy. He nodded.

"You're BP Three's friend," Tanner said. He stuck out his hand. "I'm Tanner," he said. "What are you doing around here?"

"My parents split up, and my dad lives in this neighborhood," Will said. "So I'm here every weekend."

"I thought kids from Woodville don't stoop to skateboarding." Tanner smirked.

Will smiled. "Some of us like to skateboard. But there are some people who don't like it."

Tanner knew who Will meant — the Parsons family. "They pretty much run the whole neighborhood," Will said. "But Bennett's cool, once you get to know him."

"I don't think that's going to happen," Tanner said. "Not after yesterday."

"That was a cool run," Will said. "Until you biffed, that is."

They both laughed. "Billy and I do this game where we try to match each other's tricks," Tanner said. "Want to try?"

Will nodded, and off they went. For the next several hours, the boys matched each other trick for trick at the half-pipe, the rails, the ramps, everywhere.

As four o'clock approached, Tanner saw his father pulling up to the park. It was time to go.

"That was fun," Will said. "Thanks."

"No problem," Tanner said. "You Woodville guys aren't so bad after all."

Will laughed. "I just wish the new kid hadn't ruined it for the rest of us in Woodville," he joked. "Now the only place you can skateboard is your own yard." Will and Billy laughed, but Tanner didn't.

"I was just kidding," Will said. "No reason to get mad."

"No, I'm not mad," Tanner said. "What you just said gave me an idea."

Chapter 9

Tanner outlined his idea to Will and Billy. They both liked it, but Billy wasn't sure that Will could pull it off.

"No way your dad goes for that," Billy said. "But if he does, count me in."

"Can't hurt to try!" Tanner said. "I'll see you guys later."

Tanner headed off to the car. He popped his skateboard into the trunk and got into the front seat.

"How was it? Did you have fun with all your old friends?" Tanner's dad asked.

"Yeah, it was great," Tanner said. "And a guy from Woodville was there. He comes here on weekends. His dad lives here."

They rode quietly for a while. Tanner tried to figure out a way to explain his idea to his dad. It was a big idea, one that would be tough to convince a parent to do. Tanner thought he needed to ask the question just the right way.

For Tanner, there was only one way to do it. He'd have to make a joke out of it.

"Dad," he began, "you know I love our pool, right? Well, I think I'd love it even more if it were . . ."

There was a pause. Even Tanner wasn't sure if he could say the next word.

"What?" his dad said. "If it were what? Bigger? Deeper?"

"No," Tanner said. "I think I'd love it even more if it were empty."

"What are you talking about?" Tanner's dad asked with a laugh.

"I want to have some of the guys over and have a trick contest in your pool," Tanner said. "With our skateboards."

"Hmm," his dad said. There was a long silence. "Interesting."

Tanner made every promise he could think of. They could fill it back up when it was over. They wouldn't wreck the pool edges. He would help pay for the water to refill it. Everything.

"Okay, okay, settle down," Tanner's dad said. "Let me talk to your mom about it."

That night, Tanner's parents took
him out by the pool. The water level was
already about a foot lower than normal.
Tanner knew what that meant.

"Well, your birthday is coming up,"
Tanner's mom said. "We thought it could
be a birthday party."

"This is going to be awesome!"
Tanner yelled.

Chapter 10

The Big Day

Tanner didn't waste any time spreading the news. He told Will to tell kids in Woodville who wanted to skateboard. Will said he'd bring five or six kids.

"That's great," Tanner said. "Just make sure there aren't too many. My parents said no more than ten." Tanner felt a little funny about having a party with kids he didn't know. They'd have one thing in common though, and it was skateboarding.

When the day of the party arrived, Tanner woke up early. He spent the entire morning making sure everything was just right. The pool was completely empty and ready. The snacks were all set and the drinks were in the cooler.

Now all he needed was some people.

Billy was the first to arrive. His parents drove him up from the old neighborhood. Will came a few minutes later. He had three boys and a girl with him. But no Bennett. Tanner took them into the backyard. "Where's my old pal BP Three?" he joked. "I'm surprised he's not here!"

"I didn't tell him about it," Will said. "I was afraid he'd be mad at me for coming."

Soon, the kids were zipping up and down the walls of the pool.

At first, the Woodville kids were a little shaky. Some of them didn't skateboard much, and they didn't want to try anything too risky.

Tanner and Billy showed them how to do some simple tricks. Before long, they were flying around, trying one-eighties and even harder tricks. They hooted for one another's great moves and helped one another when they fell.

After a while, Tanner sat down on the patio and took in the scene. "Looks like you made some friends," his mom said. She smiled. "Are we ever going to have a swimming pool again, or is this a skate park now?"

"We'll have a pool again," Tanner said, "because we're going to have a skate park in Woodville before I'm through."

"I don't know about that one," Tanner's mom said. "You'd have to convince the committee, and that won't be easy."

"I know," Tanner said.

"Speaking of the committee," Tanner's mom said, "where is that Parsons boy?"

"He doesn't like me much," Tanner said. "Will didn't even tell him about the party."

"That's weird," his mom said. "I could have sworn I saw him outside the fence holding a skateboard a little bit ago. I thought he was on his way around to the back gate."

Chapter 11

Tanner bolted up. He ran for the back gate and went out. No one was there.

"Are you sure you saw him?" he asked his mother.

"Yes," she said. "Maybe you and Will should go look for him."

Tanner grabbed Will and told him what happened. They headed toward Bennett's house. As they turned the corner to the park, they couldn't believe what they saw.

There, at the top of the Curves, was Bennett Parsons III. He had a skateboard! Will started to call out, but Tanner stopped him. "Shh," Tanner said. "Let's see what he does."

The boys stayed hidden by a bush. At the top of the hill, Bennett rocked the board back and forth, taking deep breaths.

He looked ready. Then he stepped up on the skateboard and started down the Curves. He wobbled a little before he even reached the first turn. But around the first turn he went.

Slowly, Bennett made his way down the Curves. A couple of times he slowed the board so much that he nearly stopped. But he never fell, and the last few turns, he took pretty quickly. When he reached the final straightaway, he pumped a fist in the air, just as Tanner had done.

Chapter 12

Suddenly, Tanner and Will saw Bennett a little differently from how they had before. They broke out from behind the bush and cheered.

"Yeah!" Will said. "Woo-hoo!"

"Way to go, BP Three!" Tanner yelled. "That was awesome!"

Bennett stopped cold. "What are you two clowns doing here?" he asked.

"Oh, relax," Tanner said. "You were at my house, so we came looking for you."

"I didn't know you could skateboard," Will said excitedly.

"Yeah, and I didn't know you were cool," Tanner joked.

"I don't skateboard," Bennett said.

Tanner laughed. "Um, I think you just did!" he said.

"Well, I wanted to try it," Bennett said. "I did it. Now I'm done."

"Man," Tanner said, shaking his head. "You have to learn to lighten up."

"Come back to the party with us," Will said. "It's a blast."

Bennett thought about it for a second.

"Well," he said, "it did sound like you guys were having fun back there."

Bennett returned to the party with the boys. He wasn't ready to use the deep end of the pool like a half-pipe.

But he did start out in the shallow end and go back and forth a little bit.

As the day went on, Bennett loosened up.

He learned that skateboarding was really pretty fun, especially once you got good enough to try a few tricks.

"Having fun?" Tanner asked Bennett late in the day.

"Yeah," Bennett said. "This is great."

"It's even better when you're at a real skate park," Tanner said.

He had a little gleam in his eye. "We should see if we can get one built here in Woodville."

"Fat chance," Bennett said.

"Why not?" Tanner said. "There's plenty of room over near the Curves. And if we all had a place we were allowed to skate, we wouldn't have to skate anywhere else."

"Good point," Bennett said. "Hmm, let me think."

* * *

Bennett and Tanner spent the next few weeks launching their plan to raise money and convince the committee to build a skate park in Woodville.

Tanner knew it wouldn't be easy to get the committee to agree. But with Bennett on his side, he thought he had a chance.

In the meantime, he made some plans with his friends, both new and old.

"Hey, Tanner," Will said. "My dad said you can stay with us on weekends if you want. Then you can skate at your old neighborhood park!"

"Great!" Tanner replied. "And when my new neighborhood park is ready, we can trade off weekends!"

About the Author

Bob Temple lives in Rosemount, Minnesota, with his wife and three children. He has written more than thirty books for children. Over the years, he has coached more than twenty kids' soccer, basketball, and baseball teams. He also loves visiting classrooms to talk about his writing.

About the Illustrator

When Sean Tiffany was growing up, he lived on a small island off the coast of Maine. Every day, from sixth grade until he graduated from high school, he had to take a boat to get to school. When Sean isn't working on his art, he works on a multimedia project called "OilCan Drive," which combines music and art. He has a pet cactus named Jim.

Glossary

ally (AL-eye)—someone who's on your side

challenge (CHAL-unj)—something that is hard or requires extra work

committee (kuh-MIT-ee)—a small group of people who make decisions for a larger group

confidence (KON-fuh-dents)—having a strong belief in yourself

convince (kuhn-VINSS) —to make another person or group of people believe or agree with you

covenant (KUHV-uh-nent)—an agreement or promise to do something

manicured (MAN-uh-kyurd) —when something is trimmed perfectly

motionless (MOH-shun-less) —not moving

promoted (pruh-MOH-tid)—moved into a new, more important job

protective (pruh-TEKT-iv) – guarding a person or thing to keep it safe

Skateboarding Terms

180 – a turn in which the skateboarder starts out facing one way, and makes a half-circle in the air

360 – a turn in which the skateboarder makes a complete turn in the air

Grind – to ride the skateboard along a surface, such as a curb or railing, by having it slide on the bottom of the board instead of the wheels

Halfpipe – a skateboarding surface with two curved ramps that face each other, connected by a flat surface. Above each ramp is a landing deck.

Kickflip – a trick in which the skateboarder flips the skateboard over and lands back on it

Ollie – a trick in which the skateboarder leaps up into the air, and the skateboard appears to cling to his or her feet

Ramp – an inclined surface for skateboarding

Tail – the back end of the skateboard

Discussion Questions

1. How could Tanner have tried harder to fit in to his new neighborhood at first?

2. Tanner likes to be a smart aleck. Can you think of some times in this story when he shouldn't have acted that way?

3. What reasons should Tanner and Bennett use to convince the committee to build a skate park in Woodville?

4. When Bennett challenged Tanner to ride the rails at The Curves, why do you think Tanner agreed?

Writing Prompts

1. If a new person moved into your neighborhood, how would you treat them? How would you try to make them feel welcome?

2. In this story, Tanner had to adjust to living in a new city. Write about a time in your life when you had to adjust to a difficult new situation.

3. Moving away from Billy was hard for Tanner. He stayed in touch by using instant messaging. How would you stay connected to your friends if you moved away?

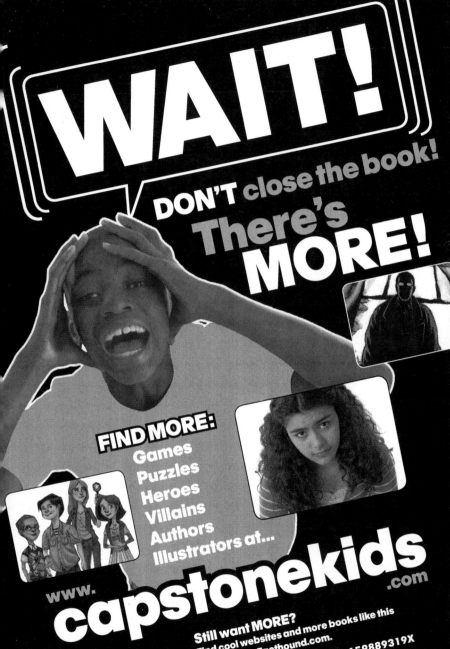